FAR OUT
FAIRY TALES

raintree

a Capstone company — publishers for children

THE GOOD FAIRY

YETI

THE BAD FAIRY

Raintree is an imprint of Capstone
Global Library Limited, a company
incorporated in England and Wales
having its registered office at 264
Banbury Road, Oxford, OX2 7DY –
Registered company number: 6695582

www.raintree.co.uk
myorders@raintree.co.uk

Text © Capstone Global Library
Limited 2017
The moral rights of the proprietor
have been asserted.

Designed by Hilary Wacholz
Edited by Abby Huff
Original illustrations © Capstone 2017
Illustrated by Alex Lopez
Lettering by Jaymes Reed

ISBN 978 1 4747 2805 8
20 19 18 17 16
10 9 8 7 6 5 4 3 2 1

British Library Cataloguing in
Publication Data: a full catalogue
record for this book is available from
the British Library.

Printed and bound in the United Kingdom

SLEEPING BEAUTY, Magic Master

A GRAPHIC NOVEL

BY STEPHANIE TRUE PETERS

ILLUSTRATED BY ALEX LOPEZ

On her thirteenth birthday, she *will* fall under my curse!

The Good Fairy now knew what to give Aurora.

I give you the gift of magic.

Aaaah ha ha!

The fairy swept her protection spell into a cloak and wrapped it around the baby. The garment would help keep the princess safe.

One day, you will defeat the Bad Fairy's curse.

You will become a *Magic Master!*

SWOOOSHHH

In time, Aurora learnt to use her magic.

Stir!

Sort of.

Eek!

PWOOOSH

Good try!

Fluff!

Whoops!

No problem!

WHOMP WHOMP

Sp-

Um, let's skip this one.

But...

25

Tales of
a sleeping princess
date back as early as 1528.
Although none of them include
a spell-casting heroine, they do
include plenty of curses!

In the 1697 version, by French storyteller Charles Perrault, seven
fairies are invited to celebrate a princess's birth. As the feast begins,
an eighth, older fairy arrives who no one had remembered to invite.
Six of the fairies grant the baby gifts of beauty, grace, wit, dance,
song and music. The old fairy, angry about being forgotten, casts a
curse - the princess shall prick her hand on a spindle and die. But the
seventh good fairy still has her gift. She softens the curse. Instead of
death, the princess will sleep for one hundred years.

Sixteen years pass. One day, the young princess finds an old woman in
a tower using a spindle. This woman didn't know that the king had long
ago forbidden spindles. The princess pricks her hand and falls into a deep
slumber. The seventh fairy returns to the castle and puts the kingdom
to sleep so the princess won't be alone when she wakes up.

One hundred years later, a prince hears the legend of the sleeping
princess. He finds his way to the castle and inside discovers the girl.
Overcome by her beauty, he kneels beside her bed. Just then, the
hundred-year enchantment ends and the princess awakens. (In the
version by the Brothers Grimm, a kiss breaks the spell.) Soon after, the
rest of the kingdom wakes, and the prince and princess marry.

Most retellings of Sleeping Beauty's tale end with that lovely picture.
But Perrault's story has a second part. In it, the prince's mother is an
ogress. The wicked ogress plots to cook and eat the
young couple's son and daughter.
When the ogress's plan is
discovered, she throws herself
into a vat of vipers.
Happy ending indeed!

A FAR OUT GUIDE TO THE TALE'S MAGICAL TWISTS!

In the original tale, fairies bless the baby princess with special gifts, like beauty and grace. In this story, the Good Fairy gives Aurora awesome magic powers!

Instead of taking a hundred-year nap, Aurora goes on an epic quest to save her slumbering kingdom!

A kiss breaks the curse in the original story. But in this far-out version, a miracle potion made of the rarest ingredients saves the day!

Aurora doesn't lie around waiting for a prince to help her. Instead, she rescues a long-lost prince!

1

The space between comic panels is called the gutter. Why is the gutter turning from white to black? How does it connect to what's happening in the story? What happens to the gutter after page 31? Why?

2

Were you surprised that the Yeti was really the long-lost prince? Look back through the story, and write down at least two text clues and two visual clues that hinted at this secret.

3

Hide.

SWOOP!

At the start of the book, Aurora had trouble with magic. Do you think she's a magic master now? Why or why not?

Sp-

Um, let's skip this one.

But...

4 Why does the Good Fairy tell Aurora to skip the spinning spell? If you need help with your answer, think about what happened when Aurora tried to cast the other spells, and also think about what happens in the original tale. Why do you think the creators included this scene?

What does the Bad Fairy think Aurora is feeling in this scene? How do you think Aurora is actually feeling? Talk about the reasons behind each of your answers.

5

HA! Silly girl, you've failed once again!

After mixing, let potion sit for three seconds...

AUTHOR

Stephanie True Peters worked as a children's book editor for ten years before she started writing books herself. She has since written forty books, including the New York Times bestseller *A Princess Primer: A Fairy Godmother's Guide to Being a Princess*. When not at her computer, Peters enjoys playing with her two children, going to the gym or working on home improvement projects with her patient and supportive husband, Daniel.

ILLUSTRATOR

Alex Lopez became a professional illustrator and comic-book artist in 2001, but he's been drawing ever since he can remember. Lopez's pieces have been published in many countries, including the UK, USA, Spain, France, Italy, Belgium and Turkey. He's also worked on a wide variety of projects from illustrated books to video games to marketing ... but what he loves most is making comic books.

GLOSSARY

convince get someone to agree to do something

curse evil spell meant to harm someone; to cast an evil spell

defeat beat or win victory over something or someone, such as in a war, fight or contest

disintegrate break up or destroy

disturb bother or interrupt someone

ingredients items that are used to make something (like a miracle potion!)

potion mixture that is meant to have special or magical effects

protection something that keeps a person or thing safe from harm

quest long, often difficult, journey made in order to find something

steed fast horse (or dragon!) that a person rides

wicked very evil, bad or unkind

willingly when you do something willingly, you're happy and ready to do it